TILL YOUR FEET BLEED

RAYNOR RUBEL

This book is dedicated to
Teddy Rubel, Alice Miceli, and Ernestine Costa.
And to all of those who read this and realize this is you,

I thank you.

CONTENTS

CHAPTER 1

Hey, how ya doin'? My name is Patrick, but everyone calls me Buddy. This is the story of how I discovered a dream I never knew I had. I also found out how to work my butt off even though I fell on it a bunch of times.

My story begins in my hometown of Newark, New Jersey. In this city, we all live right on top of each other. There's no spaces between the houses. We play baseball in the street and have to run to the sidewalk if a car comes down the road. We ride our bikes everywhere cuz all of us live close by. We have a park that has the most beautiful cherry blossom trees in the whole world. People actually travel here from far away to see them. In our neighborhood, you don't even need a phone to call your friends. You can just yell out the window and at least one of your buddies will hear you. The best is when it snows. You can't move your car until you dig it out. When the snow is good and deep, we all go sledding in the park. Every Saturday, my dad and I go to Wendy's. Of course, I got the 10-piece chicken nuggets with sweet and sour sauce, and he got the Baconator. What is cool is that the Wendy's we eat at was where he used to make the French fries. It was my dad's first job. He would remind me of that every time we went. When we got home, we'd take the little green army men out of my toy box and have a pretend battle. Of all my buddies, he was my best friend.

All the kids in the neighborhood loved to do fun stuff. We would have snowball fights every winter. We'd do rock, paper, scissors to pick team captains, and the captains picked the teams. I can run fast so I'm always a top pick along with my buddy, Nick, who has a good throwing arm. Sometimes my dad would join in, too. But he was an easy target to hit since he was so tall.

Yeah, Newark is the best. I live with my mom, my sister, Nikki, and my grandparents. My grandpa is a World War 2 veteran. He comes from what people call the greatest generation. Grandpa lived through the Great Depression. He remembers waiting in bread lines and having hardly anything to eat. He says he went from the bread line to the front line on the battlefield in Europe. He's the one who started calling me Buddy after the Buddy Poppies made by disabled veterans that you see VFW volunteers selling on Memorial Day and Veteran's Day to support struggling vets. Grandpa stays in touch with all the veterans he served with.

My dad died a few years ago. Everyone keeps telling me he's a hero for giving up his life for our country, the United States of America. He was a Navy SEAL who served on SEAL Team 3. My dad followed in my grandfather's footsteps. I am so proud and honored to be my father's son. I feel really empty without him around. I miss my best friend. I try to be strong for my mom and Nikki. Sometimes, I think they miss him more than I do. I can see the days when they are really missing him. I'll hear my mom crying at night in her room. My sister sometimes looks off in the distance and doesn't talk when someone brings up our dad. All I can do is try to be strong for them like my dad was for us when he was alive. After my dad died, my grandparents moved in to live with us. I'm glad they are with us now. I think we feel good knowing we have each other.

Life still goes on without my dad. Every day my mom goes to work, Nikki takes dancing lessons, and my grandparents take care of things around the house. And what do I do? Well, I go to school. I'm in the fourth grade. School isn't really fun for me like it is for some other kids. School is like having a headache if you ask me. I think it's because I have dyslexia. Dyslexia is when my head gets letters and numbers mixed up. Bs look like Ds sometimes and nines look like sixes. Reading and writing is just impossible some days. I'm always trying to keep up

8

with the other kids. I have days where I just don't want to go to school, but it's important to my mom and it was important to my dad, so I go. I also love seeing my friends at school.

I have three close friends: Nick, who likes baseball; Billy, who likes football; and Joe, who plays lots of video games. We have a blast together. We laugh a lot. Even though we go to the same school, I didn't start talking to Nick until I had him in the same class at Sunday school. We can't look at each other during Sunday school class or we'll make each other laugh. Nick is the one who introduced me to Billy and Joe. Ever since we met, we hang out all the time. Billy is the biggest kid in our grade at school, so no one ever gives us any problems. The other kids know that if they mess with one of us, they will have to answer to Billy. All three of them love to skateboard. It's sometimes fun but after an hour it just doesn't do it for me, man. I don't want to say that to the guys. When someone's into something, you don't want to tear it down, ya know? I wish there was something that made me happy the way skateboarding makes them happy. I tried soccer, but I didn't like that you can't use your hands. Then I tried baseball, but I couldn't hit the ball for the life of me. There was really nothing for me to get excited about doing after school, but then I heard about the school talent show. I don't know why, but it sounded like a cool thing to do. I didn't know how I could participate cuz I didn't know if I had a talent, but I always had this feeling that I could be somebody great. The idea of the talent show made me curious and excited.

Every day after school, my mom picks up Nikki and me, and we drive her to dancing school. I go for the ride cuz I have to. My mom and I wait in the lobby as my sister takes her ballet class. Usually, I just play a game on my mom's phone, unless she makes me do my homework.

One day, I decided to peek in the window of Nikki's classroom to watch them dance. While I was watching, a short, dark haired, muscular man came up behind me and tapped me on the shoulder. I jumped cuz I thought I was in trouble. I recognized him as one of the dance teachers.

I was surprised when he smiled and introduced himself. "Hey, how ya doin'? I'm Jim, one of the dance teachers here. I'm looking for guys your age to join my boys' dance class. Would you be interested in giving it a try?"

There is a boys' dance class? I completely froze. I was standing in front of the dance teacher like an icicle.

My mom jumped right in to answer for me before I nearly passed out from fear. "We'll think about it."

My mom sat me back down next to her in the lobby of the dance school. Then she handed me her phone to play games to calm me down.

On the drive home, I kept wondering if boys really danced. I had never seen that before. All I ever saw at my sister's dancing school were girls. I wanted to know more. When I thought about it, I felt sick to my stomach. My head kept going back to the idea of boys in a dance class. If all I ever saw were girls dancing, doesn't that mean dancing is for girls? And if boys do dance, what's it like? Would it be fun? Would I like it? And if I did like it, what would my family think? What would my friends at school think? You see, in my neighborhood boys don't dance. They just don't do that, but the dance teacher was a guy. What if there was a side of dance that was for guys? These questions in my head were repeating over and over.

CHAPTER 2

On the ride home, I felt kinda confused. I was so bothered by all these thoughts in my head. I felt sick to my stomach. The sandwich I ate for lunch almost ended up in my sister's hair. I walked inside, said 'hi' really quick to Grandma and Grandpa and tried to run upstairs. I think Grandpa could tell something wasn't right with me. Before I could walk past him, he asked, "Hey, Buddy, you feeling okay?"

"Yeah, I'm fine Grandpa." I could barely get the words out.

Of course, he could tell I was lying. Grandpa always knew when something was up. He gave me a look and I knew that meant we would talk later.

After dinner, Grandpa asked if I wanted some Oreos for dessert. Of course I did! But then I remembered the Oreos were in his bedroom. Now I couldn't get out of talking with him. I didn't feel like talking, but I always love going into Grandpa's room. He had it decorated with all kinds of military stuff: pics of my dad, my dad's burial flag in its special case, pics of Grandpa's army buddies, and pics from when he served in the war. He had medals, uniforms, letters in frames, and old newspaper articles from the war. He had busts of great American heroes. Busts are statues, but they're just the person's head and shoulders. He had one of George Washington and Martin Luther King Jr, plus a statue of Teddy Roosevelt on his horse. I loved looking at all the cool things

11

he had on display. It was like a museum only better cuz Grandpa is the one telling the stories and he's part of it all.

We sat eating Oreos on his bed. He asked again what was bothering me. I didn't know what to say at first. I was speechless, but then I just blurted out, "I think I want to dance."

Why did I just tell Grandpa that? He looked at me stone cold serious. I felt nervous, like I was about to pee in my pants. He took a deep breath and his expression got softer. He had the biggest smile on his face. He nodded. "My main man, that is wonderful!"

I was shocked. Did he hear me right? I actually asked him, "Did you hear what I said?"

My grandpa gave a small chuckle. "Don't you know how I met your grandma?"

I shook my head.

"I met her through dancing."

I opened my eyes wide. "Are you serious? I never knew that about you and Grandma."

He kept smiling as he told the story. "Back when I was around 19 years old, before the war, dancing was the thing to do. Every Friday night, a bunch of friends and I would go to the dance hall. It was the only way we could talk to girls. Whoever danced the best got to dance with the prettiest girl. I met your grandmother at the Camptown V.F.W. Hall in Irvington on October 6, 1939. I'll never forget the way the lights shone on her beautiful blonde hair or how her gold dress flowed out like a flower when she twirled on the dance floor." He looked up in the air as if he was remembering something. "Ahhh, the good old days." He smiled at the memory.

Grandpa got up and pulled a DVD from his drawer. He kept his top favorite movies in his room, not out in the living room with mine and Nikki's stuff. He had a John Wayne collection, but this was one I'd never heard of before. It didn't look like a John Wayne movie. It was called *Singing in the Rain.*

He took a breath and said to me with excitement, "Why don't we watch this together and then you can tell me how you feel about dancing."

We sat down right then and there on his bed, and he hit play. He pointed out the main character, whose name in real life was Gene Kelly. During the movie, Gene Kelly jumped and turned and did all these amazing things I had never seen a man do before. I was amazed. He looked like he was having so much fun while his feet were making tapping sounds along with the music. He was jumping in puddles in the rain, soaking wet, while dancing with the biggest smile on his face. Boy, did I wish I could do that. My mother never let me go out in the rain. She thinks I would catch a cold.

I was glued to the TV through the whole movie. Once it was over, I felt like I had a burst of energy. My grandpa gave me some history on it. When this movie came out in theaters, everyone wanted to be Gene Kelly. Everyone loved him, especially the girls. I asked Grandpa, "Do you think I could be like Gene Kelly?"

Without thinking for even a second Grandpa answered, "Of course, my main man. Everyone has greatness in them. You just have to discover yours. So, now the real question is, are you willing to dance til your feet bleed?"

I was shocked. I didn't expect to hear that from my grandpa. I sat really still. I just said, "Yeah, I think so."

Grandpa looked at me sternly. "Do you think Gene Kelly was just born with all that talent? Do you think he was born with the gift of being able to jump like a bird and turn like a tornado?"

I shrugged my shoulders. I didn't know what he was getting at. He answered his own question, "No. It was all hard work. That's how Gene Kelly was able to succeed. That's how he was able to be great. He didn't just wake up one day a great dancer. He worked hard every day. He believed that he could do it. You will absolutely be the next Gene Kelly if you want it bad enough and if you're willing to work for it. And I mean really work for it. Work beyond your limits and believe in yourself. And you gotta dance. Dance til your feet bleed."

I nodded and looked at his wall with all the medals. I looked up at the pictures of my dad with his SEAL team. I looked at the pics of Grandpa and his army buddies when they were really young. He continued, "And besides, you are in this great country where if you have a dream and you're willing to work hard, you can become whatever you want."

When I heard that, I knew I had to talk to Jim. I knew I had to dance.

CHAPTER 3

The next day when my mom and I took my sister to dance class, I walked straight into the building and found Jim, the dance teacher. I stood right in front of him, looked him in his eyes, and said, "I want to join that boys' class." I wasn't even nervous this time.

He smiled. "The first class is this Wednesday at 6:00 pm. Don't be late."

I nodded. I walked like I had a purpose and sat with my mom to wait for Nikki. The second I sat back down I started second guessing what I had done. My mind was spinning. Was this the right decision? What if I didn't like it? What if I did like it? Would I be made fun of at school?

When Wednesday came around, I was kind of nervous. Actually, I can't lie, I was really nervous. I didn't know what to expect, and wondering about it was killing me. I walked into the dance class and there were three other boys. We all stood around at first, just looking at each other. We were all a little nervous. It was kind of awkward. I think we were all feeling the same way, thinking the same thoughts. At 6:00pm sharp, Jim came in and welcomed us to the class. He Introduced us to each other. Right after we said our awkward 'hellos,' the class began. The class started with what Jim called a 'warmup.' He had us move parts of our body while other parts did different things. One minute we were working on pointing our feet, and the next we were bending

15

our knees. We worked our way up to rolling our shoulders and circling our heads. We even rolled out our wrists and stretched our fingers. This warmup included parts of our bodies we never even knew could be used for dancing. This was different than what I had seen in some sports where you only use certain muscles and certain body parts - like in baseball when a pitcher warms up his pitching arm only. I felt like we were warming up everything. We used every muscle that could possibly be used. I couldn't believe how hard it was, and this was only the warmup.

Once we were all warmed up, Jim showed us some dance steps. He taught us how to do them as we moved from one side of the room to the other. He called it 'going across the floor.' First, he had us doing a movement where we shuffled from side to side. We then did some spins on one leg. I liked it cuz it reminded me of something I saw Gene Kelly do in the movie. After the spinning, we started jumping, and boy, do I mean jumping. Jim kept repeating "Higher! Bigger! We don't jump in dance, we fly."

I felt as if no matter how hard I tried to get higher in the air, it still wasn't high enough to please Jim. It's as if he knew I could jump higher if he just pushed me. As we moved from wall to wall of the studio, we all huffed and puffed. "These steps are a lot like baseball drills," I thought out loud. I didn't realize how dancing gave you a workout similar to what I'd seen athletes do on the field for their warmups.

Jim chuckled at my comment then gave us some background. "Dancing was originally only for men back in the 15th and 16th centuries. The first ballet school was created by King Louis XIV in France, and it was only for men. Women couldn't attend. Actually, dancing has been around since the beginning of time. Even in the BC times, cave men danced around the fire, reenacting their hunts. Dance was how they told stories. They even had war dances and wedding dances either to celebrate or to act out how they wanted things to go."

I was really surprised by what Jim was teaching us. The history of how dance began and how it changed over time was so interesting. I wanted to learn more. Jim finished his story and we got right back to work. In the last fifteen minutes of class, Jim explained that he was going to teach us steps that went with a song. The song he

played was one I knew and liked. It had both a piano and a guitar in it. The song was "Scenes from an Italian Restaurant" by Billy Joel. Jim taught us each a different step. Then he combined them all. He called it a "combination." As we were learning more and more of the combination, it seemed as though the steps fit perfectly with the music. As my body moved with the music, the dancing made me feel powerful, like I was a superhero. The class came to an end, and I left the studio feeling free.

My mom was right there, patiently waiting for me when I walked out of the class. She asked, "So, what did you think of the class?"
I burst out, "I had a great time. It was really hard. Jim told us this story about how dance began, and I jumped really high. We danced to this really cool song and look I learned this, and..."
"Whoa, whoa, whoa." My mom put her hand up. "It sounds like you had a great time. Does this mean you'll be coming back next week?"
I made a fist and jammed my elbow back like I had just made a touchdown. "For sure!"

As we drove home, I was talking a mile a minute about everything that went on in class. When we got home, I ran out of the car and practically bust the door open. I rushed in to find my grandma and grandpa and tell them all about the class. I was so I excited. I yelled for Grandpa, "I took my first dance class! It was so cool."

Grandma grabbed me and squeezed me in a big hug.

Grandpa chimed in, "Oh, I am so happy, my main man. Show me some of the things you learned."

I rushed into the living room and started showing my family what I learned. Nikki even came down to see what moves I was doing. I felt like a million bucks with all this attention, but for some reason I just felt something was missing. I paused and looked around the room at all my family members' smiling faces. The only thing that was missing was a person. Dad. It was at that moment I wondered what Dad would have thought of me dancing. I wondered if he would've been proud of me. I guess we will never know. But my dancing was bringing joy back to my family. That hadn't happened since before my father died. It was really cool seeing everyone happy again.

CHAPTER 4

My next class was a whole week away. It felt like time was moving so slow. I had no idea what was to come, but this time I wasn't nervous at all. I mean, what was the worst that could happen? Well, in the next class, we were doing one of our combinations, and yup, you guessed it. I fell. I fell right on my butt. The second my body hit the floor, I could feel the blood pumping to my butt cheeks. My face was turning bright red as sweat dripped down from my forehead. I was so embarrassed. I was surprised no one in the class laughed or made fun of me. If it was one of my friends and they saw me fall on my butt, they would laugh and give me a hard time about it, but that didn't happen here.

Instead, Jim reached out his arm and lifted me up. "No matter what you are going to do, you are going to fail before you succeed," he said. "You should know that failing is part of anything you learn to do, so you should do what you love so you don't fail at something you don't like doing." He turned and looked at all of us boys. "All of you, listen and remember this! Most people never get back up when they fall down. They just make excuses. They blame everyone except themselves. But if you are willing to take ownership of your life and know that the only reason you're not successful is because of your actions or lack of action, then you will reach your dreams." Jim continued intensely, "When we have a dream, we need to realize that we will fail many times before we reach any of our goals. Do not let failure turn you away from your dreams. Instead use it as fuel to motivate you to achieve your dreams."

Jim's words stayed in my head. Why be ashamed of failing, when failing is just one step closer to achieving your dreams? It made falling on my butt not as embarrassing. It was just part of becoming a great dancer.

Now that I was back up on my feet, we continued our dance combo. This week was slightly harder than last, but even though it was harder, I enjoyed it even more. It was something about the challenge of trying to learn what your arms, legs, feet, and head could do separately and then in the end put them all together. It gave me a rush of energy. As I was trying a few of the steps before we did the combo to the music, I turned my head and saw my grandma and grandpa peeping in through the viewing window. They came to watch me!

Jim hit the play button and we started grooving. I think I messed up a couple of the steps, but I was having so much fun I really couldn't tell you which parts I messed up. When we finished the combo, my classmates and I thanked Jim and left the studio. The first person I saw as I walked out the door was my grandma. Right away she said, "Wow! Buddy, you can really dance. You are a natural at it."

Grandpa said, "You were moving like Spiderman in there. Some fast learner you are at picking up those moves. You are definitely way better than I was back in the day."

I was so happy to hear them say those things. The people who loved me most were proud of me. I think this was the first time in my life that I felt like I was special, like I had something that was all my own to offer to the world. For the first time, I felt as if I had purpose in my life, and the cool thing was that I could share it with others.

We headed to the car to drive home from the studio. I sat in the back, like usual, while Grandma sat in the passenger seat and Grandpa drove. Usually, car rides with my grandparents were either real quiet or real loud . . . if you know what I mean. This car ride was different though. We were all talking and laughing. Grandma told me she wanted to show me a couple old movies, and Grandpa couldn't stop humming the song I danced the combo to from class. They both went on and on about memories they had from when they were young and had danced together. I sat in amazement, just listening. So many good memories and good feelings all because of dancing.

"Hi, honey. How was dance class?" my mom asked when we got in. Before I could even get a sound from my mouth, Grandma pulled me into the living room and started showing me the waltz clog.

I didn't know what a waltz or a clog was. I knew this was going to be a mistake. And I was right. I was not the greatest waltz clogger there ever was to say it nicely. I was stubbing my toes and getting my feet all tangled in each other. After seeing how much fun I was having trying to understand what Grandma was teaching me, all of my family members joined in. It was a grand time. We were all laughing and joking. I took a second to appreciate how nice it was to see everyone so happy.

CHAPTER 5

The days of the week went by, and everything was normal: school, homework, chores. I used every free moment to put on some music and dance. I was obsessed with it. I never wanted to stop. I didn't even realize that I hadn't hung out with the guys in a while.

On Sunday mornings, we all went to church. This Sunday was a little strange. As I walked with my mom and sister, I noticed people pointing at us and whispering and kinda smiling. At first, I thought it was Nikki because she had a pretty dress on, but then I realized they were pointing at me. It seemed weird, but I thought nothing of it.

We sat down in our seats and waited for the service to start. An old couple came up to us, and the lady said to me, "You're Buddy, right?"

I answered with a cautious, "Yeah."

Then she teased, "Your grandma told me that you're gonna be a star."

I looked at my grandma. I was confused. Grandma just smiled at me. Of course, I was only feeling one thing: embarrassed. My face was red. My forehead was sweaty, and so were my palms. I looked at the old couple and just said, "Thank you." They were the only two words I could think of, to be honest. But why was Grandma telling the whole world that I'm dancing and going to be some big star? I mean, I'm so inspired that my grandma and whole family have so much faith in me, but I really was hoping they weren't going to spread it around the neighborhood, especially the church. My friend Nick came up to us, and for some reason he looked at me like he was really angry.

"What's wrong with you?" he snapped.

I was so confused. "What do you mean?" I had no idea what he was getting at.

"So instead of skateboarding with us, you go and wear a tutu and be a girly girl?"

I was upset and angry at the same time. I was mad but I also felt like a loser. I couldn't believe that I found something I really enjoyed, and now my best friend thought I was a loser for doing it. I had nothing to say.

"You have nothing to say? Listen man, I don't want to be around you no more if you're gonna be dancing!" Then he just walked away and sat with his family in the pew across from us. The rest of my family was busy talking, so they didn't notice. My only thought was how much I didn't want to go to school tomorrow. After church, Nick and his family left before I could talk to him. We went home, and I spent the rest of the day hiding in my room, wondering what the kids at school were going to do to me tomorrow.

CHAPTER 6

When I got to school the next day, it immediately went downhill. The second I walked into the building, kids were throwing things at me, and everyone was laughing. I just wanted to run away. I headed to class, but it only got worse. Kids were shouting things like "Hey, girly girl!" when I walked past them in the hall. Nick must have gotten to them. Nick even got Joe and Billy to go against me.

"Your dad's a war hero and you go and wear a tutu," spat Billy. They all just laughed and called me names. I tried my best to ignore it, but when they mentioned my dad, my insides boiled. After lunch, the bullying got even worse. They started throwing quarters at me and kept asking me to dance.

Then came a moment during class when Nick stood up and yelled, "Don't you think your daddy would be ashamed of you?"

My heart was racing; the veins were popping out of my neck. I was grinding my teeth and clenching my fists. I just couldn't take it anymore, so I was going to do something about it. I pushed my chair away from my desk as I stood up. It screeched like nails going down a chalkboard. I walked over to Nick, who had just shouted at me, and looked him straight in the eyes. Everything slowed down. I felt like I was in an action movie. I had so much anger. Without even thinking, I felt like I turned into the Incredible Hulk. I punched Nick right in face. He fell to the ground. His nose started to bleed. Nick got sent to the

nurse's office and I was sent to the principal's office. As I walked into the office, Principal Johnson was sitting in her big black chair, staring me down as if she was grabbing onto my soul. She took her finger and gestured for me to come in and sit down. I did as I was told. "Patrick," she said as she fixed her glasses.

I answered, "Yes, Principal Johnson."

"Should we ever lay a hand on another student?" she demanded.

"No," I replied in a low voice.

"Are you sure about that?" she asked even more loudly.

"Yes, Principal Johnson," I droned.

She asked me why I had done what I did. My only response was a shrug of my shoulders. Principal Johnson pried and tried to get me to explain why I had punched the kid, but my lips were sealed. Next thing I knew, I heard the office door open and see my grandpa. He looked so angry. I had never seen him this angry. *This can't be good*, I thought to myself. I could easily tell my grandpa was angry cuz his eyebrows only ever moved when he was upset, and boy, were they moving. My heart started beating fast. I had the nervous sweats. *What's in Grandpa's head? Is he going to scream at me? Am I going to get grounded?*

CHAPTER 7

My grandpa took a seat next to me, and he talked with Principal Johnson. He was stern when he said to her that this would never happen again and I would be punished for my actions. I was suspended from school for the rest of the day, which meant a scary ride in the car back home with Grandpa. I was so scared. I had never done anything this bad before. My teeth were chattering, and my stomach was definitely feeling the burrito I'd eaten for lunch.

Grandpa and I got in the car and sat for a moment in silence. This felt like the longest two minutes of my entire life. I fully believe watching paint dry would have gone by faster than those two minutes in the car with silent Grandpa. After what seemed like forever, Grandpa broke the silence and said, "You listen and you listen here, boy. You will never change anybody with your fist. It will get you nowhere except into trouble, which will lead down the path to jail. You hear me?"

I quickly nodded my head like a bobble head doll.

Grandpa then yelled, "You want to get even with those boys, then you win. When I say win, I mean win at life. You want to have revenge? Then you succeed. You follow your dream. Do what you love. You have to realize everyone is going to have something to say about what you do. The only people you listen to is your small circle. That is your family and close friends. Everyone else, don't pay any attention to! You want to get even with those kids who are saying mean things?"

"Yeah, I do, Grandpa."

"Well, then you win," he said.

"How do I do that, Grandpa?" I asked.

"You get stronger, smarter, and most importantly, you do what you love. You don't want to be doing something you hate your whole life. You will be miserable."

"But what if they keep bullying me, Grandpa? Aren't I supposed to do something about it? Stand up for myself?" I asked in a genuine voice.

Grandpa shook his head and in a warm voice said, "You just remember that these bullies are too scared to dance themselves. You have courage to try something new. They will never be brave enough in life, and instead they just put others down to make themselves feel better. You see this right here?" Grandpa took his hand and placed it on my heart. "This is the path you follow. It will guide you exactly where you need to go. It really hurts me that these boys think dancing is shameful and embarrassing. Actually, I've never told you who taught me how to dance, have I?" he asked.

I shook my head.

"His name was John Fort. He was with me in the 16th Regiment when we stormed Omaha beach. He could dance better than Gene Kelly," Grandpa explained.

My eyes went wide. "He could dance better than Gene Kelly?"

"When he did the Lindy Hop it was like watching an MGM movie. Folks would clear the dance floor and let him and his partner have the floor."

"Where is Mr. Fort now? Do you think he would want to teach me to dance?" I wondered.

Without a response coming from his mouth just yet, my grandpa's eyes filled with tears. He pulled the car off to the side of the road to explain the rest of the story. He dabbed his eyes with his handkerchief. "We were in a Higgin boat. Those are the types of boats we used to storm the beach during the war. I was standing right next to John at the time. We were happy that we weren't part of the handful of men who were throwing up from the roughness of the sea. You could hear guys praying out loud. They knew what was coming right in front of them. We heard 30 seconds! The whistle blew. The door opened and we charged forward. Bullets came flying towards us. John got shot in the shoulder and at that very moment threw me into the sand. He told me to stay down. John then realized that our staff sergeant and sergeant had both been killed. We looked around and saw most of our platoon dead. Then John yelled, 'Forward!' Next thing I know, I see a bullet hit John in the leg. He was screaming because of the pain. It was astounding how he had been shot twice and was still willing to fight strong. I yelled 'Forward' to any other men who were still alive. We were getting closer to the German bunker. John then tells me to get by the dune and give him covering fire. Meanwhile, John and seven other soldiers charged the bunker." Grandpa was getting more emotional as he told the story. He took out his hankie again.

My grandpa stopped for a second. It was so quiet in the car. Then tears poured from his eyes, and I heard the sound of pure sorrow. I had never seen this amount of emotion come out of my grandpa. The only other time I saw something close to this was the day of my father's funeral. After a few minutes, he got control of his emotions, wiped his eyes, and went on with the story. "John charged with the seven other soldiers to the German bunker as a few men and I gave them covering fire. John only got about 4 feet before he was ripped apart in pieces by the German MG 42 machine gun. Seeing this I just dropped my gun and ran out and grabbed John's body and dragged it back by the dune. By the time I got back to the dune, John was already dead. I just broke down and cried right then and there holding his body in my arms.

"Buddy, let me tell you. John was the greatest dancer I ever knew and the strongest, bravest, and most courageous man I've ever known. If it wasn't for him throwing me into that sand, I would have died. He saved my life. There's not a day that goes by that I don't think about him, that I don't feel grateful for the life I was given to live because that man saved me. I'll tell you something. He would have been so proud of you dancing. I am sure he is proud from wherever he is now. So, when those boys make fun of you or say mean things, you remember John. You remember how strong he was, not only for your grandpa, but also for his country.

"There's something very important I learned while in the army, and that is you can't control what happens to you, but you can control your reactions. And you have to be in control of your emotions. When you are angry, you cannot let it control you. When you are sad, you cannot let it eat you alive. A person who is strong never gives in and is always in control. Is that understood?"

"Yes, Grandpa."

He pulled the car back on the road and we drove home. At home, my grandma and mom were sitting at the kitchen table. I was sure they were waiting to yell and scream at me, but before they had the chance Grandpa told me to go to my room. As I walked towards the stairs that led to my room, I overheard Grandpa explaining everything to both my mom and grandma. He told them to take it easy on me and that I had been through a lot today. I didn't want to listen anymore; the more I listened the more I felt disappointed in myself. I just had to be strong and in control like Grandpa had just taught me. Tomorrow would be a new day.

CHAPTER 8

The next morning, I got up extra early. I had spent the entire night thinking about what Grandpa told me in the car. If I wanted to get even with those boys, I knew I had to win. I kept thinking about how he told me to follow my heart. Then it hit me. For first time in my life, I knew what I wanted to be when I grew up. I wanted to be the next Gene Kelly. That's how I would win. My head started racing. I knew I had to talk to Jim. He was the dance teacher who could make me the next Gene Kelly. I spent the entire morning thinking about what I wanted to say to Jim. I prayed that he would believe in me and help me. I asked my mom to take me to the dance studio so I could talk to Jim. I felt nervous and excited at the same time.

I left the house and headed for school with my head held high. When I got to class, Nick and the guys started up again, except now they had three girls with them. They started with, "Hey, twinkle toes. Do you want to kiss me, Buddy? Are we feeling like a princess today?" They all laughed and made kissing noises, except for one of the girls. She had beautiful dark brown hair and big blue eyes. Her name was Valerie. She sat two seats behind me in homeroom. I had a crush on her since the first grade.

Valerie looked upset at the boys for making fun of me. "Guys, stop. It's not funny," she scolded.

I was shocked that she defended me.

Nick got angry at her. "Why? You ever hear of a boy that dances? That's what girls do."

All of them were angry at her. Valerie didn't know what to do, so I went and sat with her as the rest of them continued to tease me.

It was so hard, but I did my best to ignore them. I just kept repeating to myself "to get even is to win. To get even is to win." My grandpa had never steered me wrong. I knew I had to hold on tight to what he told me so I could have the patience to wait for them to stop all this bullying. I had some doubt as to when that time would come, but I knew Grandpa always had my best interests at heart. He would always tell me the truth. I had to trust that. Besides, my dad and John Fort were watching over me from above. I had to make them proud.

Our teacher, Mrs. Miller, said half-heartedly, "Cut it out, boys." It really bothered me that Mrs. Miller let it happen in the first place. Instead of bringing Nick and the boys to the office, she just let it happen.

It made me think, *Does she think they're right? Does she think dancing is not for boys?* I felt my body shake and I just wanted to scream. It felt like a terrible nightmare, but I knew I had to stay strong and not give in. I couldn't let them get to me. I had to stay focused on me and my dancing. I must win!

After school my mom to took me to the dance studio. Even though it wasn't Wednesday, she knew I needed to talk to Jim. It was urgent.

"Hey, man. What are you doing here? It's not Wednesday, is it?!" Jim said jokingly.

"No, it's not Wednesday, but I really needed to talk to you," I said seriously.

"Sure. What's up?"

"I want to be one of the greatest dancers to ever live, like Gene Kelly. Do you think it's possible?" I wanted to know what he thought.

Jim looked at me very seriously. He took a long pause before answering, "Yes. It's possible. You have the potential to be great. But you must be willing to out-work everyone. Second, you must understand that the best doesn't always get the job. You could do hundreds of auditions and still not land a job even when you are the best dancer there. If you understand that and are willing to take that risk, then I don't see any reason why you couldn't be one of the greatest."

I took one step closer to Jim to let him know how serious I was about this and asked, "What do I need to do?"

Jim waved me on, "Come with me." I followed him into his office. He sat me down. "So, now if you really want to be like Gene Kelly, we have to get you a good foundation of technique. We will have to get you into at least four ballet classes a week, a jazz class, a stretch class, a contemporary class, a tap class, and a partnering class." He was saying all these things so fast. I didn't understand everything, but I listened like my life depended on it.

"We also need to get you proper shoes: ballet, tap, and jazz shoes. Is your mom here? We should bring her in to discuss all of this."

I walked outside to get my mom from the car. There was a moment where I second-guessed what I was doing, but once I thought of how proud my grandpa would be, all my worries went away. My mom and Jim discussed all the different classes I'd be taking, what the schedule would be, and what gear I would need. My mom is very good at math. She figured out in her head how much this would cost. She looked a little nervous. "This all sounds wonderful, Jim, but I don't think we can afford all these classes. With his sister already enrolled and our family only having one salary, I just don't think I'll be able to come up with the money."

Jim smirked with a mischievous grin. He knew something my mom and I didn't. He explained that all of this would be at no cost. Completely, 100% free. All we'd need were the shoes and he could get us a discount. My mom and I could hardly believe it. What was the catch? His only condition was for me to do everything I could to be the greatest dancer that I said I wanted to be. My mom's face lit up. She couldn't stop thanking Jim for his generosity. Jim explained how there really weren't enough boys in dance and thought maybe if I danced, it would inspire a new generation of boys to want to dance too. My mom and I left the studio feeling overjoyed and blessed. My grandpa was right. I didn't give in to those bullies; I stayed focused on myself. Now Jim was giving me free classes. I felt like a winner.

CHAPTER 9

The next class couldn't come soon enough. When it did, I danced my heart out. It was like I did each step with more excitement than I ever had. The next morning, I woke up to my mom's voice saying, "Buddy! Buddy! Get up! You need to be in the shower in the next five minutes. You stink!"

I rubbed my eyes and tried to get out of bed. I could barely walk. Each step felt harder than the last. I was so sore. I groaned on my way to the bathroom. When I finally made it there, I held onto the wall as I got in the shower to "de-stink" as my mom would always say. It felt like I was moving extra slowly cuz of how sore I was. After cleaning up, I got dressed, ate some breakfast, and barely made it to the bus on time. The bus ride was quiet. I could sit there in pain from my sore muscles without having to deal with any of the mean kids. For some reason, when it's the middle of the week and people are tired, they cause less trouble, even though at school Nick, Billy, and Joe kept up their usual once we got to class. Valerie was sitting two seats behind me. I could see that she was bothered by what the guys, who were supposed to be my friends, were doing to me. But I didn't let them see that it was getting to me.

On the car ride home, I told Grandpa about the dance class, but I mostly talked to him about Valerie. I told him I didn't know what to do

and what to say now that it looked like she was paying attention to me. It wasn't for a good reason, but she still noticed me more than she ever had since the first grade. Grandpa laughed out loud.

"You should just be yourself, kid."

"What do you mean?" I didn't know who else he thought I would be.

"Well, if she doesn't like you for who you are, then she's not the right one. You should never have to change yourself to make someone like you, and that goes for life in general. People wonder why they are so unhappy, and it's because they're not being themselves."

"Okay, but I still feel nervous talking to her." I needed more of a plan.

"Well, Buddy, if you don't talk to her then some other guy will. And you will be the one who loses out," he warned.

"Alright. I will do my best."

"There you go, my main man. Remember, just be yourself."

I still wasn't 100% sure what that meant.

Once I got home, I started thinking about what questions to ask her. Maybe I should ask her how old she was or what school she wants to go to someday. And then I thought, *I'm just going to wing it and be myself.*

CHAPTER 10

The next day at school, there was a flyer on the bulletin board about the school's talent show. The audition was two weeks away. My heart was beating double time, I was so excited.

I'm going to audition, and I'm going to win the talent show with my dancing. After school, I asked my mom what she thought about it. She was excited. She told me that it was a great idea, but I should ask Jim first and hear what he had to say.

When I got to dance, I asked Jim about it. He thought it was an awesome idea. "Ya know, Buddy, we have a tap teacher here on Thursday nights named Mel. He can choreograph a dance piece for you that could help you win the talent show."

I was a little confused. "I thought you would teach me."

"I could, but Mel will get you to perform your best as an artist."

"Artist? What do you mean by that?" I wondered out aloud. "I thought an artist was like a painter or something."

"Well, it's like when I told you that anyone can do a dance step. But it's how you do it that makes you a great artist. Plus, Mel worked with great people like Arnold Schwarzenegger."

"You mean The Terminator?" I was excited.

"Yup. Him and Gregory Hines."

"Gregory Hines? Who's that?" I'd never heard of him.

"Oh gosh, well you'll have to look him up on YouTube when you get a chance. He's one of the greatest tap dancers that ever lived."

"As great as Gene Kelly?" I asked.

"Oh, yeah." Jim nodded. "But you gotta understand, he doesn't teach just anyone. He will only teach people he believes have the potential to go professional. Maybe he could come in Wednesday to watch you dance and give his opinion."

"Okay." I was very nervous. Would Mel reject me? If Jim believed Mel could get the best performance out of me, then I definitely needed Mel to choose me. If he rejected me, did that mean I couldn't be a professional dancer? *I just have to wait for Wednesday and hope that he'll work with me.*

CHAPTER 11

Wednesday finally came. I got to the studio and wanted to throw up, I was so nervous. The class started, and Jim was warming everyone up. Suddenly, the door banged opened. There was a man in his 70's wearing wing-tipped shoes, dress pants, and a black sweater with a huge smile on his face just standing there in the doorway. He waited for Jim to realize he was there. When Jim saw him out of the corner of his eye, he ran to the stereo and shut the music off. He turned toward the door. "Man, you must be getting old! I didn't think you were gonna make it."

The man gave a friendly laugh. "Why, you shut up before I slap you in the back of your head." Both of them started laughing as they hugged.

"This is Mel," Jim said proudly. "He'll be observing our class today. Mel is not only one of the best teachers we have here, but in my opinion one of the greatest dancers that's ever lived." When Jim said that I felt my stomach start twisting. Jim clapped his hands. "Alright guys, let's go across the floor."

During the whole class, Mel would either have a super intense face as if he was going to fight us or he would have a giant smile as if he were in Heaven.

I wasn't really sure how he felt. The class ended. I felt I could have danced better. Jim said we did a good job and he'd see us next week.

As the other boys left the studio, I stayed behind. Jim closed the studio door, and Mel stood up. He walked over to me. "Hey, kid, I want you to tell me how you feel when you dance."

I didn't know what to say. I had to really think. My heart started beating faster. Then it just came to me. "When I'm dancing, I feel like I'm not me. I feel like a superhero. When the music starts playing, I just feel like I need to move. It's like my legs are moving on their own. When this happens, I'm just so happy. I don't know if that's the right answer, but it's the truth."

Mel laughed. "There is no right answer."

Jim walked over. "So, Mel, what do you think?"

Mel took a knee and got eye level with me. He looked like a cop about to question me. "Well, you made a lot of mistakes in class. For your age, you're very behind." I felt so discouraged. Then Mel smiled. "But you got IT, kid."

I fired right back at him, "What do you mean by IT?"

"IT means the gift," Mel explained. "It's when people watch you and you put a smile on their face. Most people can't do that. Now even if you have the 'IT' factor, that still doesn't make you a great dancer. Your body has to be in shape like an Olympic athlete, and that ain't easy. If professional dancing was easy, everybody would do it. Besides that, when is that audition for the talent show?"

"Not this Friday, next Friday." He jumped up as if there was a fire. "A week and a half? That is no time at all." He shook his head.

Jim interrupted him. "Mel, you remember that time when I helped you with that audition?"

Mel seemed frustrated. "You never seem to let me live that down."

"Well, you booked that movie with my help. Isn't that right?" Jim reminded him.

"Alright, alright, but I need Buddy to rehearse with me, every day after school for an hour, at least." Then there was silence, but Mel was smiling like he knew something.

"So, you're gonna help me with the talent show?" I wanted reassurance.

"Yes, I will," said Mel, nodding sincerely.

"How much will you charge to teach me?"

Before Mel was able to answer, Jim said, "Don't worry about that, Buddy. Mel and I will work that out."

Mel put out his hand to shake.

"Awesome!" I said and shook his hand.

"I'll see you after school in studio 2."

I said, "Okay."

"One more thing: what's your favorite music, Buddy?" he wanted to know.

"Classic rock," I answered. I went to the waiting room and told my mom the good news. She was so happy for me. I just felt so lucky that Mel was willing to take me on as a student.

The next morning at school, I was so proud to sign up on the talent show audition list. Nick and his minions, Billy and Joe, walked by. When they saw me signing my name, Billy knocked the pen out of my hand. Nick got in my face. "I can't believe I was your friend. Now you're gonna put a tutu on and dance in front of everyone like a fairy. What a loser!" Both Billy and Joe laughed and walked away. I was trying not to give in. I just thought of Mel and how he was going to help me win the talent show. *I'll show those guys what dancing really is and how awesome I am at it. I'm so tired of being walked all over and being called names, made to feel like I'm worth nothing. I can't wait for the audience to go crazy for my dancing. Mel said I had IT.*

That day felt like it dragged on for so long. I couldn't wait to hear the bell go off so that school would be over.

CHAPTER 12

When I heard the school bell go off, I grabbed my jacket and backpack and tried to avoid Nick and his minions. I rushed to my mom's car. When I got to the studio, Mel was dressed all in black. He had these boots on that looked almost like cowboy boots. "Mel, can you dance in those boots?"

"Why yes, I can. When I was in the shows *Chicago* and *Sweet Charity*, that the great Bob Fosse choreographed, he always wore boots. So, to honor him I wear these boots."

I didn't know who Bob Fosse was, but I didn't want to admit I didn't know him. I changed the subject. "Jim told me that you worked with The Terminator."

"You mean Arnold Schwarzenegger?" Mel asked with a twinkle in his eye. I nodded. Mel laughed. "When you're in the business as long as me kid, you meet a lot of people. On another note, I never asked you . . . what do your parents do, Buddy?"

"Well, my mom is an accountant. And my dad, well, he died fighting for our country. He was a Navy SEAL," I said sadly.

"I'm so sorry to hear that, Buddy. I am so thankful for his service. If it wasn't for heroes like your father, we wouldn't have the freedoms we have today." Then Mel patted me on the back. "Okay, enough chit chat. We got a lot of work to do and no time at all. So, I'm thinking we do a dance where you are in a leather jacket and jeans to the song

'Pinball Wizard' since you said you like rock music. Jim and I will create a guitar that you can dance with. It will light up, and it will have a handle, so you're able to spin the guitar around as part of the dance."

"Oh, that's awesome!" I was super pumped.

"Oh, one more thing. You're gonna have to get knee pads."

"Knee pads?" I was confused.

"Yeah. I'm gonna have you do a power slide."

"A power slide?" It sounded cool.

"Don't worry, just trust me."

Mel started showing me steps. He was going so fast. He noticed I was getting upset because I wasn't able to pick up the steps fast enough.

"You want to be a great dancer?"

I nodded.

"That means you have to pick up the steps fast. So, take some deep breaths. The more you dance the faster you'll learn to pick up steps. Think about when you were a baby and every time you fell, did you just cry and not get up? No, you picked yourself up cuz if you didn't, you wouldn't be able to survive. That's just like dancing. Be patient with yourself. One day you'll be impressed with how fast you can pick up the steps . . . true story."

I thought about it. I told myself to be patient and not to get so frustrated with myself. By being patient and sticking with it, learning the steps did get easier. When my mom picked me up, I was so tired. I went right to bed after dinner.

CHAPTER 13

The next two days of rehearsals with Mel went well. I was shocked at how much I had memorized. When I was finishing the class with Mel on Friday, the back of my heel was in pain like it was burning. When I stepped on it, it felt like a knife was cutting through it. I screamed and fell to the floor. Mel rushed over to me. I took my shoe off. You could see blood through my sock. Mel took my sock off to look at it. The back of my heel was bleeding. I thought of what Grandpa said. Are you willing to dance till your feet bleed? Well, it looks like I did.

Mel looked at it and said softly. "You're okay, Buddy. It's just a blister. Let me go get you a band-aid." Mel cleaned and dressed the wound for me. He told me to go easy and not push too hard in the dance till it healed up. All I could hear was my grandpa saying to push through it. It's the hard work that makes a great dancer, like Gene Kelly. When I heard the music, I pushed through the pain and gave it my all, even though Mel had told me to go easy. I felt like a champion by dancing and not giving into the pain.

Mel looked at me with a serious expression. "That's one of the best times I've seen you dance, but you still have a lot of work to do. We're gonna take Saturday off. Sunday we'll start again."

"Thanks so much, Mel." I was feeling proud.

"See you Sunday, kid. Oh, tell your mom to stick your foot in Epsom salt with warm water. It will it help heal." He winked and smiled.

CHAPTER 14

On Saturday I slept in. I woke up at 11 am. I was shocked; I had never slept in that late. My body was really worn out. I tried to stand up to get out of bed. My feet felt as stiff as rocks. I was so happy today was a day off from dancing. I really needed it. When I was watching my favorite movie, *Godzilla*, I did what Mel told me and put my foot in warm water with Epsom salt that my mom had fixed up for me. I did it four different times during the movie. It really did help my foot feel better. Mel told me a part of exercising is always being sure to have rest. He was right because on Sunday I could jump higher and spin faster. That one rest day made my body feel so much better.

In Sunday's lesson, Mel gave me the guitar that I was going to dance with. It was awesome! The guitar was green and red. It was made of wood and had a small handle on the back. I asked him what the handle was for. He showed me how I could make the guitar spin, but that wasn't the best part. I saw that there was a light switch on the back. When I flicked it, the whole guitar lit up. All I could think was that when I auditioned for the talent show the judges were going to love the guitar. I gave Mel a big hug and thanked him.

"You're welcome, kid. A rock star always needs a guitar."

"Thanks, Mel." I was so happy I gave him another hug.

CHAPTER 15

The next day, Mel was really hard on me. He kept making me run the dance over and over again. He wasn't happy with how I was dancing the routine. He kept saying, "You can do more, kid." Or he would ask, "If this was the last time you were to dance, is that how you would do it?"

I felt so annoyed and angry. "I don't get what you want from me!" I yelled. The room was silent, and my fear set in. Was Mel going to yell back at me?

"When you perform, you have to express yourself. Dancing isn't just movement. It's movement with feeling. What I mean by expressing yourself is being you and nobody else. Own that stage! Don't be afraid of what others will think. Give it your all. For instance, I'm going to teach you the Mountain Dew technique."

"What the heck is that?"

"This time when you dance, I don't care how bad it looks I want you to pretend that you drank three Mountain Dews and you're going crazy from the sugar." He wasn't laughing.

"You can't be serious." I thought he was crazy.

"Do it!" Then Mel walked back to the stereo. The song began. I imagined that I drank three Mountain Dews. I pretended I was having a sugar rush. I couldn't stop smiling. It might sound crazy, but it felt

like l was dancing on clouds. I stopped worrying about the talent show and whether I was doing the steps right. I was just having fun. When I finished the dance, Mel looked at me with the biggest smile.

"Mountain Dew technique always works!" he laughed. "You see kid, when you stop thinking and just stay in the moment, you can be yourself. That's when the real art comes out. That's why we dance. True story!"

Mel looked at me with approval. I felt like Spiderman when he got bit by the spider and now had superpowers.

CHAPTER 16

I trained hard for the rest of the week, and Thursday finally came. It was my last class with Mel before my audition. Mel went pretty light on me and just kept reminding me to have fun. Whether I made it or not, I least I'd know for sure I had worked hard. After class he told me, "Wait here." He smiled like the Grinch who had something up his sleeve. He left the studio for a few minutes and when he came back, he had two Mountain Dews. He opened them up and passed one to me.

"Cheers. I think you're going to make it big time, kid."

"Really?" I was shocked that he said that, knowing Mel. He was very hard to please.

With a big smile he said, "I'm proud of you, kid. You said that you would show up and work hard every day, and you did. Most people won't do that. They say a thing but don't follow through. They don't do what they say they will, but you did."

It felt good to hear him say that.

"You're going to really give those judges a show they'll remember. Close your eyes and take a deep breath. I want you to imagine you're performing the dance in front of the judges. Picture yourself

performing for them. Imagine you're dancing really well and really feel the joy you get from that. Then you hear the judges tell you that you got in the talent show. Now take a deep breath and open your eyes. Remember to close your eyes and take a deep breath before you dance. This is your time. You're going to do great. True story!"

CHAPTER 17

During school I felt really nervous, as if I was going to war. I kept looking at the clock on the classroom wall, waiting for the day to end. Finally, I heard the bell ring. I knew it was go-time. I put my books in my bag and headed to the gym for the audition. When I got there, there were over 50 kids all warming up or practicing for the audition. There was one kid juggling. Another girl was dancing. One girl was warming up on her flute. It sounded and looked like the Macy's Thanksgiving Day Parade, except all the floats were deflated and nobody knew who was first in line for the parade.

I even saw Valerie and her friends. Valerie had on a gymnastics leotard. I didn't even know she did gymnastics. I kept staring at her till we made eye contact. She waved to me, and I got red in the face. I didn't know what to do, so I just looked away. I felt so silly.

Then three of the teachers from school who were going to be the judges walked in. They set up a table and called everybody one by one to come to the table and get a number. They said that when our number was called, we'd get up and perform our act. They also told us only 20 of us would get to perform in the talent show. I got number 49. I was second to last. I was kind of angry because I had to wait a long time with the nerves I was feeling. It would be easier to be one of the first to perform so I could just get it over with. Valerie got number 2. Lucky her. When she was performing, she put me in a daze. With all her tricks

and grace, I knew she would get in. Then I realized I had to perform in front of everyone that I was competing against. The pressure was on. To be honest I wanted to throw up, but as students kept coming up and performing their acts, a couple of things were popping in my head. One thought was, *what happens if I fail?* Then I thought about Nick and the guys bullying me all the time. I thought about Valerie, knowing she was going to watch me dance. I thought about the excitement I gave my grandparents when they saw me dance for the first time. They would be disappointed if I didn't get in the show. *Will Mel be upset if I mess up the dance?* Then I thought about my dad and I got really sad, but of anyone, I knew I had to give it my all, for him.

"Number 49," one of the judges called. "Who is number 49?"

"That's me," I said nervously.

"You're up, kid. Go get on the stage."

CHAPTER 18

When I got on the stage, one judge asked me, "What will you be performing for us today?"

"I will be dancing to the song 'Pinball Wizard'."

I set up my guitar, closed my eyes, took a deep breath, and thought of Mel. I thought to myself, *I'm going to give them a performance they will never forget.* The music began playing. I was a little shaky in the beginning, but I thought about the Mountain Dew technique and to just trust myself. Most importantly I knew I had to have fun. I started dancing like never before. For the first time, I really did feel like Gene Kelly. I had this feeling of greatness, but I couldn't tell if the students or judges liked the dance. When I pulled the guitar out, turned the lights on, and started spinning it, you could hear the students start oohing and ahhing. When the song finished, almost everybody in the room started clapping. Even two of the judges were clapping. I had a gut feeling that I would be one of the top twenty.

I sat down and watched the last student do his juggling act. It felt like time was dragging on. Then the judges told us to give them five minutes and they would call the numbers that would be performing in the talent show. Waiting for those five minutes was so nerve wracking. I felt as if I was in a horror movie. My heart was beating so fast. The judges stood up and started calling the numbers. "Two, six, twelve." I was happy for Valerie. She was number two.

I realized that if I was called, I would be called last. I was waiting and waiting, and then I hear the number 46. *Please call my number. Please call my number.*

"Number 49 and 50 as well," called the judge.

I jumped up for joy. It was like Willy Wonka, and I got the golden ticket to the chocolate factory. The judge thanked everyone for coming. She told all the students to come to the audition next year for those that didn't get in. Turning to my right, I saw Valerie point to me and say something to another girl. Valerie looked at me like I was a superhero. I didn't know what to do. I had never talked to a girl before, other than saying 'hi.' I grabbed my guitar and backpack and ran to my Grandpa's car yelling, "Grandpa, I did it!"

"You got in, buddy?"

"Yes!"

My grandpa looked so happy, as if he was the one who got into the talent show. I could tell he was so proud of me. He then told me it was time to celebrate. "Let's go get some cannolis." Cannolis were my favorite dessert. I think they're better than any cake I've ever had. This was one of the best days of my life. I just couldn't wait to tell Mel tomorrow that I got in.

CHAPTER 19

I told Mel what had happened at the audition. Mel thought it was great that I got a shot to perform in front of people before the competition. He asked me when the talent show would be. I told him it was next Saturday.

"Well, Jim and I will be there."

I felt so honored.

He continued, "For the rest of the time, we'll keep rehearsing but realize all of the work has been done. We just have to keep you in dance shape."

On Monday, the school posted in the hallway all of the names of the people performing as a reminder in case someone got confused or needed to know the time of the performance. It listed everyone in the school who would be performing. It was in hope of getting more kids to go to the talent show. As I was looking at the poster, Nick and his minions came by.

"I guess you'll be showing the whole school on Saturday how much of a girly girl you are," teased Nick.

Then a group of five girls walked by, including Valerie. "Hey, we saw you at the audition. Your dancing was amazing." Valerie blushed. I was shocked. She thought I was good. The girl I had crush on for years. Holy smokes!

Nick looked confused. "You like him dancing?"

"Of course. He was like Zac Efron," one of Valerie's friends gushed. Then the other girls began blushing and giggling.

"You were so cute when you danced yesterday," another girl said sweetly.

Billy looked amazed as he watched the girls flirting with me. In disbelief he said, "Hey, maybe I should start dancing."

Nick looked at Billy with a confused, angry face. "Billy, what's wrong with you!?" Nick just walked away. He seemed mad. The funny thing was that Billy and Joe stayed. The girls continued talking to me. They asked what type of dancing I did and all different dance questions. Out of all the girls, Valerie seemed the most interested in me. When she and the girls were asking questions, I gave short answers. I really didn't feel confident. I was pretty red in the face. Talking to Valerie made my heart beat so fast. I was so excited that the girl of my dreams was talking to me. Joe and Billy just stood there like deer in the headlights. They were in a state of shock. In mid conversation the bell went off, and we all walked to our classrooms.

During school, I was kind of upset. Don't get me wrong, I got in the talent show. The girl of my dreams was talking to me, but I just felt like I wasn't myself. I felt like I was too shy. When I got home, I would have to talk to Grandpa. He would know what to tell me.

At the end of the day when I was putting my books in my bag, Billy approached me. "Hey, Buddy, do you think I could come with you to one of your dance classes?"

Did I just hear that right? "Are you joking? All this time you made fun of me, and now you want to join me?" I laughed in his face and walked away. I couldn't believe it.

Billy chased after me. He was red in the face, like he was embarrassed. "I'm serious, Buddy. I really want to learn dancing. Seeing all those girls talking to you and having a crush on you, I thought it was at least worth a shot."

I didn't say anything and continued to walk away, shaking my head.

Billy pleaded, "I'm sorry, man. I'm really sorry. I don't know what was wrong with me. I shouldn't have listened to Nick."

I stopped and looked at him. I always believed in giving people second chances. I mean, look at Darth Vader. He saves Luke at the end of the movie in Return of the Jedi. He throws the evil Darth Sidious into the Death Star's reactor. It was Darth Vader who saves the galaxy in that moment. So, I had to give Billy at least one more chance.

"If you want to join me, the class is on Wednesday night. We can go together." I reached my hand out and we shook on it.

CHAPTER 20

When I got home, I went right to my grandfather's room. I first told him about Billy wanting to join the dance class. He was just as surprised as I was. But as he told me, that's what happens when you win. You inspire others.

Then I went on to what I really wanted to tell him about, which was Valerie. I told him I didn't know what to do or what to say. He laughed out loud.

"You should just be yourself, kid." He had said that to me before.

"What do you mean?" I asked impatiently.

"Well, if she doesn't like you for who you are then she's not the right one. You should never have to change yourself to make someone like you, and that's also for life in general. People wonder why they're so unhappy, and it's because they're not being themselves."

"Okay, but I still feel nervous talking to her."

"Well, Buddy, other than John Fort, who I told you saved my life in the war, I always gave credit to my Drill Sergeant, Drill Sergeant Houston. He not only prepared me to fight but prepared me for life.

It was our second day of training. Drill Sergeant Houston yelled at all of us to get to our attention. One of the guys in our boot camp was Luke McNeil. When Sergeant yelled, Luke stood looking clueless without his feet even together." Grandpa burst out laughing. He could barely get a word out. "Well, Buddy, Drill Sergeant got in his face and

said some mean words that I don't want you to know, but I'll never forget what he said after that. He said, 'I bet you've never been on a date with a woman. And you know how I know? Your shirt is untucked. You don't stand tall with your chest out. You look like a scared kid. I see fear in your eyes. How are you gonna get a date and what woman is gonna marry a loser? Now if you don't want to be a loser, you better get your act together.' Then I heard Sergeant yell the loudest I ever heard him yell."

Grandpa got in my face for this part of the story and pointed his finger, reenacting Drill Sergeant. "'Do you want to be a loser for the rest of your life?'" Grandpa yelled at me as if I was Luke. Grandpa scared me. I had never heard my grandpa yell like that. "'No sir!' Luke yelled back at the Drill Sergeant. Drill Sergeant replied, 'That's what I like to hear because you will never end up getting married. Even worse, we're not going to win this war. Losers don't win wars. It's the men who stay strong and never give up no matter what the situation is, they are the ones who win in war and in life. One more thing, Luke. After we win this war and you go back home, you must go on a date with a girl, cuz girls like winners, but you gotta act like one. So, you better learn to tuck that shirt in, stand up tall with your chest out, and tell her how you truly feel. Your days of being a loser are over.'"

Grandpa softened his voice. He showed me how to tuck in my shirt. Showed me how to stand up tall with my chest out. I stood in front of the mirror and smiled. "Buddy, now you go do what Drill Sergeant taught me. Be yourself and tell her how you feel." I felt really powerful and ready to talk to Valerie with no fear.

"You got it, Grandpa!"

"There you go, my main man."

True story, I thought. *True story.*

CHAPTER 21

Wednesday came; Grandpa and I picked up Billy at his house. When Billy got in the car, he seemed kind of nervous. I think he was afraid, like I was when I first started dancing. Or maybe he was afraid of what Grandpa would say to him after he and the guys had bullied me for weeks, but Grandpa didn't bring it up.

In class, Billy sat in the studio watching me work with Mel. I could tell Billy was fascinated by it all. It was the first time he ever saw dancing in a studio. After I finished with Mel, the studio door opened, and Jim came in. He saw Billy and had a look of surprise. "Are you joining our class?"

Billy looked so scared, as if Jim was a monster. Billy looked very shy and responded, "Yes, I'd like to."

Jim had a huge smile. He almost looked like he was going to cry, he was so happy. It's kind of rare to have a boy so interested in dancing, and here I had brought him another one. His idea was catching on. Jim started the warmup. Billy didn't do bad in the warmup, but he struggled going across the floor. I looked at Billy, and I told him not to get in his head.

"I just hope this dancing impresses the girls because man, I feel like a fool. I didn't realize how hard dance is. This is harder than football."

"Just stick with it, man. You won't feel that every time you dance. It will get easier," I reassured him.

Then we got to the combo. Jim was teaching us this new jump that none of us had learned before. I couldn't believe it. Billy actually got it on his first try.

Jim was shocked. "Hey, guys, let's stop for a minute. I want to point out Billy is bigger than all you guys, so it's gonna be harder for him to get in the air." Jim looked at Billy intensely. "Billy, I'm really proud of you. You're giving 110%. You're going all in. And if everybody in this room goes all in, you all can be great dancers."

I could tell that boosted Billy's confidence. After class, Billy walked over to Jim. "Hey, I'd like to sign up for the rest of the semester."

"Awesome!" Jim shook his hand and pointed Billy to the front desk to sign up. When Grandpa came and picked us up, Billy limped over to the car.

"Billy, you alright?"

Billy was a little out of breath. "Man, I feel so sore. It feels like I ran two miles," he sighed.

"At least your feet ain't bleeding," I announced. "Last week my feet were bleeding cuz of my blisters."

He nodded. "Yup, I didn't realize dancing was this hard." Then Billy told Grandpa how cool he thought dancing was. Billy didn't understand why dance was thought of as something that's not for boys, seeing that it was tough and demanding like football. He said he wished he started dance when he was younger so he could be like Jedi in dance. It was cool seeing how much Billy enjoyed dancing after Nick bashed it so bad.

CHAPTER 22

The next day in Mrs. Miller's class, Billy limped over to me.

"Man, I'm so sore. I'm gonna ice my feet when I get home."

Nick and Joe came up to me trying to make another joke, but Billy got in front of me. "Cut it out, Nick."

"What?!" Nick looked angry and confused. He tried to get around him, but Billy is a big boy.

"Cut it out!" yelled Billy. All it took was one step to the side to block Nick's way.

He said it so loud he sounded like he was gonna fight Nick. The classroom got silent.

"Boys, what's going on?! Everyone take your seats," Mrs. Miller said sharply.

Billy winked at me and gave me a fist bump, "I got your back, man."

At lunch Billy sat with me for the first time in weeks. A girl came up to our table. Her name was Samantha. She had blonde hair in a messy bun and big beautiful blue eyes. She said she was a dancer. I told her that Billy was dancing now, too. Samantha started talking to Billy about dancing. They got into a deep conversation. I could see Nick and Joe a couple of tables away staring down Billy and me, giving us dirty looks. For the first time, I felt bad for Nick and Joe. Billy and I were winning in life. We were taking chances, facing our fears, following our

dreams. Nick and Joe didn't want to take a chance to follow their own dreams, so they took their lack of confidence out on us. They weren't happy so they wanted to make other people unhappy. It's just really sad. As much as I had a lot of anger about it, I still felt bad for them.

CHAPTER 23

My last class with Mel before the talent show was my favorite class with him. We ran the number and worked on corrections, and then ran it a few more times. We were just making sure everything was super crisp and clean. Mel said, "Hold on one minute." He walked out of the studio. I started to get in my head, and fear set in. I was afraid of messing up, disappointing my grandparents, and being laughed at when I danced. After all this hard work, I was afraid of losing the competition. Mel came in with his Mountain Dews and gave me one. He saw in my face there was something wrong.

"Buddy, you looked like you saw a ghost. What's wrong?"

I just let everything out like a train off its tracks. I told him everything I feared.

"Buddy, Buddy, calm down. We all have fears. I have fears just like that. It's called being human. You're going to feel what you're going to feel, but you have to use that fear as excitement and channel it into joy. Remember, you have been practicing this dance so much that it's in your heart. You have to trust yourself that when that music starts playing your body will do the dance naturally. Just have fun out there. Buddy, this is what you love to do. This is not what you fear to do. This is your opportunity to share that love. Tomorrow is time for you to play and have fun. I know Jim told you about the movie I was in, Total Recall. When I was auditioning for it, I wasn't worried about anything.

I was just having a good time and being the character. Even when I made the final callbacks, I still didn't let anything get to me. I decided I was going to have a good time. Remember, kid, we all have fear. It's okay to fail and make mistakes in life, but never lose to fear. Channel fear to joy and you will achieve whatever you put your mind to. True story!"

I stood there just listening and taking everything in. It felt good that he understood me. "Thanks, Mel."

"I can't wait to see you perform. We are all so proud of you," he said sincerely.

CHAPTER 24

I woke up the next morning feeling like crap. I thought that since it was the day of the competition, that I would wake up happy, but I had a nightmare that night. In my nightmare, I was performing and my dad was there watching me. Then he just disappeared. I woke up feeling so sad. My dad will never get to see me perform. When I went downstairs, Grandpa had my chocolate pop tart on the table with a glass of milk. I sat down, and after two bites of my pop tart I just started crying.

"What's wrong, Buddy?"

I just kept crying. I tried to get the words out of my mouth, but it was so hard to just say it out loud. I took a deep breath. "I wish Dad was coming today."

Grandpa got sad, too. He took a deep breath and put his arm on me. "In war, you will never know why people die for no reason. When I got home after the war, it took me years to come to my senses. I kept asking God, 'Why did I get to live and not my brothers?' We all had families and were good people. They were just like your dad. But, Buddy, you must know that your dad will be with you today, I promise you. He will be watching from Heaven. One way that helped me recover after the war was by making every day count, honoring your dad and all that have fallen. Everything I do in my life is for them and their sacrifice for this country. I could tell you right now your dad is so proud of you. When you get on that stage and dance for him, he's going to be smiling up in Heaven."

Grandpa and I hugged. "You better get all your stuff for your performance."

I finished my pop tart and milk and got ready. When I got to school there was excitement in the air. Everyone was pumped for the talent show. I felt this energy, like it was Christmas day, and I was waking up, about to open all my presents. I was just so excited. I headed to the gym carrying my outfit and my guitar. *It's time to get my game face on and give everyone the show of a lifetime.*

CHAPTER 25

I entered the gym and my jaw dropped. I couldn't believe what I saw. They transformed the gym. There were over five hundred seats and they had put up a stage. One of the teachers said, "Hey, Buddy, go behind the stage. Get in costume and set up your stuff before any of the audience gets here."

I went backstage. All the other students were getting ready. One girl kept making these bird sounds. I guess she was doing that to warm up her singing voice. One guy was juggling. One guy was doing punches and kicks for his karate demo. I saw Valerie stretching on the floor. She looked so excited to see me. She stood up and gave me a big hug. "Good luck! You're going to do great in the show."

I didn't know what to say. I had never been hugged by a girl before other than my mom and sister. I got really red in the face and almost couldn't get a word out. "You too," I said, embarrassed.

"Thanks," she said with a big smile. Then Valerie went back to stretching.

I set up my guitar on the side of the stage and put my jazz shoes on, and most importantly my black leather jacket. When I put the jacket on, I felt so cool, like I could take on the world. People started entering the gym and the judges told us to get backstage. I just kept thinking of what Mel told me to do: channel that energy into joy and remember the Mountain Dew technique.

I went to the side of the stage and one of the teachers showed me the sheet with the order the performers were going in. I was to perform in the middle of the show, so I felt pretty good. At least I was not last, and it was right after Valerie's performance. Then the people in the audience took their seats. It was a mostly full audience.

Then the show finally began. The audience went dark and one of the judges came out on the stage to the mic. "If everyone could silence their cell phones now, thank you. At the end of the show, we will be giving out our first, second, and third place medals for the top three best performances."

The judge headed to his seat next to the other two judges. One of them announced, "Now performing is Tiffany Lee, who will be playing the flute." After she finished her song, the audience clapped, and she bowed.

Then the next performer came on stage. Some performances got a loud applause, and some got a soft applause. Some people messed up their performances, and some did better than they did in their auditions. Some people were really happy after they performed, although one girl came off the stage and burst into tears.

Finally, Valerie got called up. Watching her on stage was like seeing an angel. I was crushing on her so hard. She bowed and the audience loved her.

When I heard, "Next up, Patrick Dolton performing a dance to 'Pinball Wizard,'" I snapped out of it. My heart started beating so fast I thought it was going to come out of my chest. I started to sweat and felt very hot. I walked onto the stage. I looked out into the audience.

Instead of people, all I could see was black. I couldn't even recognize anyone because of the stage lights shining in my eyes. As much as I knew people were in the audience, I had this feeling of being alone, almost helpless. My body even started to shake. It was like I was stuck in the mud; I couldn't move. So, I remembered what Mel taught me. I took a deep breath and said to myself, *this is my time.* Then I heard the music begin to play.

CHAPTER 26

Once I heard the first note of the song, Mel was right. My body just started dancing. The cool thing was it almost felt like everything was going in slow motion. I gave the dance everything I had in me. I felt like a rock star. I felt free, like I was a Jedi using the Force, or Spiderman when he shoots his web and swings from building to building. I grabbed my guitar, and the lights on the stage dimmed. I turned the switch on my guitar and started spinning it. I heard some, "Oooohs" from the audience. I felt the audience was loving the dance. I did my power slide with the guitar and went into my ending pose. I felt so out of breath, like I'd just run a marathon. I bowed.

There was just silence.

I got in my head, seemed like I really didn't do that well. I felt that I did an amazing job in the dance, so why the silence?

Within seconds the audience not only clapped but got up out of their seats and cheered. The audience was roaring. I felt like a star. I tried looking for my family, but I couldn't see them because of how bright the stage lights were. It was amazing to hear people clapping. Some people were even yelling, "Bravo!" I took a second bow and walked off the stage. I felt so happy. I wished I could do it again. I felt like after that performance, I was absolutely going to win first place for the talent show.

After the last student performed, all three judges came out onto the stage with three trophies. The first place trophy was my height with

gold on it. The second place one was half that size with silver on it. The third place trophy was almost the same size as the second but had no silver on it.

"Ladies and gentlemen, thank you for coming to this year's annual talent show. Let's have another round of applause for all our performers. Now to announce the winners of this year's talent show."

I started praying that I would win first place.

"Third place goes to Tiffany Lee for playing her flute so wonderfully." The audience applauded for her. She smiled and took her place on stage holding her trophy.

"In second place, we have Patrick Dolton for his dancing."

I was shocked. This can't be real. I felt so disappointed. How could I have not won first place? I thought I did an amazing job. I went up to the judges to get my second-place trophy. I tried my best to fake my smile, but I felt so bad. I should have won first; it was so unfair. The audience loved me.

Then they announced, "Teddy Smith wins first place for his juggling."

They gave a huge loud applause for Teddy. I wanted to just run off the stage. I put so much hard work in for this performance and I lost. I mean, second is the first to lose. I felt like a real loser. All that sweat in the studio, dealing with all the bullying, all the pain, and I lost. I just wanted to break down and cry.

But then the lights turned on in the audience.

And I couldn't believe what I saw.

CHAPTER 27

Mel and Jim were sitting in the front row on the right. I saw my grandparents, mom, and sister in the center in the third row. I looked to the left and saw a group of five older guys my grandpa's age wearing veteran's hats. I realized those guys were my grandpa's war buddies. These were the soldiers who fought in World War 2 with him. These were the men he had told me stories about night after night for all these years. I couldn't believe my grandpa's friends came to see me. These were war heroes – the guys from the pictures. It was so awesome! All these people came to see me! I headed off the stage with my trophy in my hand. Although, I was still sad about getting second place.

Mel and Jim walked up to me with big smiles on their faces.

"That was the best I have ever seen you dance," said Jim.

"So how do you feel?" asked Mel.

"Well, I really wanted to win first place."

I almost wanting to break down and cry. Mel went down on one knee and looked at me intently. "Kid, life ain't about the prize or victory or an award. It's about the journey. You will realize that the enjoyment you get is not from the trophy. It was all from those hours spent in the studio trying to better yourself, trying to be the best you. You will realize in life it's working toward the goal that makes you happy, not achieving the actual goal. All that trophy is going to do is stay on your shelf and it's probably going to get thrown out eventually. But you're dancing; that's going to be with you for life. And it's going to make you money one day. More importantly, your dancing will make, and has already made, people happy."

"Yeah, I guess you're right," I agreed.

"True story," said Mel.

I saw my family. My grandma gave me a big hug and started crying and telling me how great I did. My sister smiled and gave me a big thumbs up. Then my mom hugged me so tight that I couldn't breathe. It was really cool seeing how proud my family was of me. My grandpa said, "Hey, Buddy, look who came to see you."

My grandpa motioned to his war buddies. The first man came up to me. He was super short and wearing a blue dress shirt with tan chinos. "Wow, you can dance! You were like Gene Kelly up there," he said with a huge smile.

I didn't believe him. Did my grandpa tell him to say that? "Are you sure?" I asked.

"Listen, when I was a teenager, I used to go see all the Gene Kelly movies, and I'm telling you, you move just like him."

I was so happy to hear that. "Thanks. Gene Kelly is my favorite."

Then the three other veterans shook my hand and congratulated me. The fourth guy was 6'3. He was like a skyscraper, but he was built like a Viking. He had a chin that looked like it was made of steel. He just looked so mean and ready for a fight. My grandpa brought him over to me. "Buddy, this is Drill Sergeant Houston."

I was so scared. I quickly put my feet together, my arms down, and my chest out. I stood at attention.

"At ease, young man," he said in a deep voice. He sounded like Batman. "I know you love dance, Buddy, but you would make one great solider. With your hard work and courage to get in front of a crowd like that, you would make one great solider. Your grandpa talks about you a lot. He is really proud of you. And I'm proud of you too."

I was in shock that Drill Sergeant Houston said that to me. I mean, he trained some of the best warriors the world has ever seen. "Thanks, sir."

Then I saw that on my left was Valerie. I quickly tucked in my shirt and walked tall with my chest out toward her. I gave her a big hug. "You were amazing!"

She started blushing with a huge smile. "Buddy, you were so awesome up there. You were good in the audition, but in front of the audience, you were on fire!"

"Really?"

"Yes. You were like a Disney prince and rock star put together."

"Thanks."

"Also, you should have won first place."

That made me feel really good.

And then I thought about Drill Sergeant and my grandpa and knew I had to say what I felt. "Hey, next week you want to get ice cream with me?"

Without any delay she answered, "I would love to." Then she gave me a big hug.

I turned around and saw Drill Sergeant Houston. He gave me a thumbs up and winked at me. I did the same back to him. Then I heard him tell my grandpa, "You taught your grandson well."

"Hey, it's what you taught me."

Drill Sergeant Houston then patted Grandpa on the back. I told Valerie that I'd talk to her later. I walked back over to my grandpa's war buddies.

"Well, thanks for coming," I said sincerely.

"We are so happy your grandpa invited us," said Drill Sergeant Houston, answering for the group.

I looked at my grandpa with a big smile. He patted me on the back. I just looked around at my family, friends, and teachers and realized what my grandpa was talking about, having a small team of people who support you. Then I took a moment and realized Mel was right. Through this journey, I learned to face my fear. I found something I really loved to do. I got amazing teachers in my life. I made a date with a really cool girl, and hey, I even got Billy to sign up for dance. Thinking about all those hours working my butt off in the studio, it all added up to today. All I could think was that it was so worth it. We all walked out of the gym, and then I heard somebody call my name. I looked around. There was no one so I kept walking. Then heard it again

"Buddy!"

I turned around and it was Nick and Joe. I felt so angry. *What are they going to do, make fun of me again?*

CHAPTER 28

My grandpa turned around as well and got really angry. "What do you gentleman want?" he asked with authority. He gave them a look like a cowboy about to have a gunfight. The two of them looked so scared. They both looked at my grandpa and then at me.

"Hey, Buddy, I totally get it if you don't want to forgive us after everything we did and said to you. But we are really sorry, man."

I just shrugged my shoulders. To be honest I really didn't know what to say to them. It felt good to hear them apologize, but at the same time I still had anger towards them.

"We really didn't know what dancing was, but, man, you were so cool up there. No wonder Billy started taking a class with you. Plus, you should have seen all the girls watching you. They looked at you like you were a pop singer. It was just awesome," said Nick.

Joe stayed quiet and was nodding to what Nick was saying. Then Nick extended his hand out to me. I shook his hand and then Joe extended his and I shook it as well. Then I told them, "I appreciate it."

I wasn't too sure what else to say. I mean, it was nice that they said that, but I still felt pain from everything they did for the past few weeks. But hey, maybe we can start with a clean slate. My grandpa looked at me with a big smile while the boys walked away.

"You see, just like I told you . . . when you win in life, focus on yourself, and follow your heart, that's what happens."

Mel came up to me. "Alright, we got to get going, kid. Will I be seeing you on Monday?"

"Yes, of course."

Then Mel got really serious, "Good, because you've got a lot to learn, kid. You almost fell out of that turn." He smiled and winked at me and gave me a hug. Jim gave me a hug, too, and they both left.

"Alright, Buddy, let's go. We got cake at home to celebrate," said Grandpa.

"And cannolis too?" I asked, really pumped.

"Of course! They're your favorite!"

Today couldn't get any better. My family and I headed home and celebrated with cake and cannolis. We talked about the talent show and all the acts, which ones my grandpa liked and which ones my sister liked. We had so many laughs. My mom was so happy. She hadn't been this happy since my dad was alive. I knew Dad was smiling at me from Heaven. It was so nice seeing her have so much joy from my performance.

After we celebrated, I took a shower and headed to bed. I started thinking. This is a day I will always remember. Thinking about all the hours dancing, my struggle trying to talk to Valerie, competing in the talent show, missing my father and pushing through the pain, and getting bullied almost every day for dancing. Knowing all this, I faced it head on. I followed what my heart told me. And even when I didn't win, I knew the real way to win was by learning and making myself better.

I believe I do have a shot at being one of the greatest dancers to ever live because I know I'm willing to work hard for it. I'd be willing to have my feet bleed every day, and this is only the beginning.

I cannot wait to see what new adventures I will go on, and the new challenges I will face.

But what I know is . . .

I'm ready.

True story.

Acknowledgments

I want to thank all those who helped
inspire and bring this book to life:

Professor Lisa Sargese
Nicolette Rubel
Lia Capasso
Mike Capasso
Mel Johnson Jr
Jeff Shade
Jim Raposa
Claudia Shell
Nicholas Garr
CorBen Williams
Brian Crowe
Christina Rubel
Kirk Rubel

About the Author

Raynor Rubel is a theater and film actor who also teaches performing arts to kids with special needs. At 9 years old he tagged along with his sister to dance class and dreamed of one day being on stage himself. After achieving his dream, he opened Carousel of Progress Academy whose mission is to provide a place for kids with disabilities to express themselves through dance, drama, and martial arts.

CPSIA information can be obtained
at www.ICGtesting.com
Printed in the USA
BVHW060341181122
652194BV00003B/181